GAHAN WILSON'S
MONSTER
PARTY

"Gahan Wilson is like a box of chocolates. Wait long enough and you'll get maggots and spiders. That's because cartoonists Wilson, Chas Addams *(The Addams Family)* and Gary Larson *(The Far Side)* are masters of macabre humor." —*Suspended Animation*

ALSO AVAILABLE
Published by ibooks, inc.:

Gabon Wilson's Gravediggers' Party
by Gahan Wilson

THE MAD READER SERIES
The MAD Reader
MAD Strikes Back!
Inside MAD
Utterly MAD
The Brothers MAD
The Bedside MAD
Son of MAD

GAHAN WILSON'S
MONSTER PARTY

GAHAN WILSON

ibooks
new york
www.ibooks.net

DISTRIBUTED BY SIMON & SCHUSTER, INC.

A Publication of ibooks, inc.

An ibooks, inc. Book

Distributed by Simon & Schuster, Inc.
1230 Avenue of the Americas, New York, NY 10020

ibooks, inc.
24 West 25th Street
New York, NY 10010

The ibooks World Wide Web Site Address is:
http://www.ibooks.net

ISBN 0-7434-7987-4
First ibooks, inc. printing October 2003
10 9 8 7 6 5 4 3 2 1

Edited by Steven A. Roman

Cover art copyright © 2003 Gahan Wilson

Cover design and color by Arnie Sawyer
Interior design by Joe Bailey

Printed in the U.S.A.

GAHAN WILSON'S
MONSTER PARTY

"Why aren't you out there protecting
us from evildoers, young man?"

"Somehow, somewhere along the line, this town lost its pride."

"I've passed your complaints along to the captain."

"*Your Honor, the defense contends its client could never get a fair trial in this court.*"

"You <u>stop</u> it now!"

*"Give me the number of the Snappy Pop
Bang Cereal Company, please!"*

"I'm sorry, Mrs. Smith, but our tests show your child is a changeling left by the fairies."

"We're just going to have to be patient, gentlemen."

"Wake up, you idiot—you forgot to turn off the hat."

"As my late husband, here, used to say. . . ."

"Of course, the place wouldn't seem so small if we weren't elephants."

"You've been to one of those punk-rock places again, haven't you?"

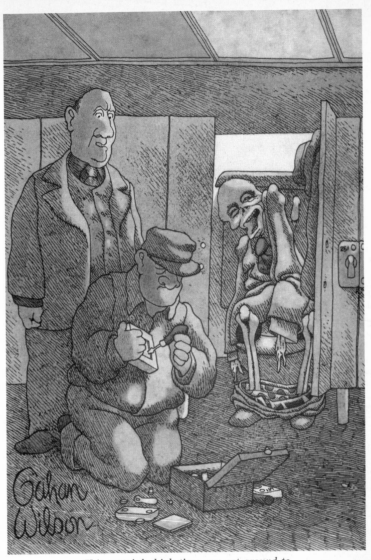

"It's certainly high time you got around to fixing that lock, Straus!"

"*You could learn a thing or two from Harrington, here, Wiltz.*"

"It's true, of course, that I'm just a machine,
but I do have a built-in vibrator."

"Occupant, apartment 5C: Congratulations—you
may already have won the all-electric Colonial
split-level house of your dreams . . ."

"What do you say we give Chief Wapapatame here another of those
Thanksgiving punches before talking over that little land deal?"

"We've heard the rumors, ma'am—there's absolutely nothing to them."

*"How many times I got to ask you to
go easy on the stops?"*

*"Has the defendant anything to say before this court
passes sentence?"*

"I guess it's some kind of an orgy!"

"I'm afraid our expedition has been a trifle too successful, professor."

"Surely, Nurse Greer, you must have had _some_ suspicion
Mr. Appleton was no longer here!"

"I'd tell you how I do it but it'd only spoil the trick."

"Surely it can't be midnight already."

"I'm coming! I'm coming!"

"Oh no—_not_ him again!"

"I told you this lake was completely untouched."

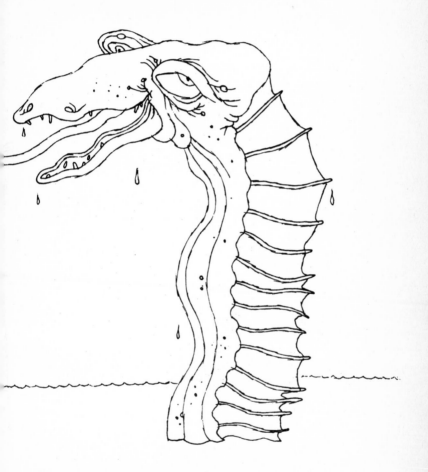

"One wonders what he would have done had he lived longer."

"I knew you'd like that one, Sir."

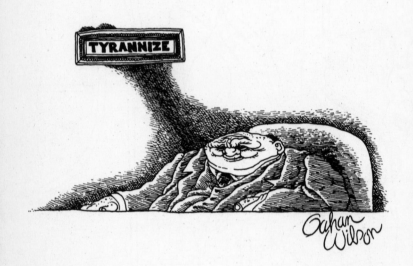

"*Don't be a stranger, now that you know the way!*"

"I'm just not sure the general public is ready for this, Foster."

"Anyone here seen Swaxee's head?"

"*Of course, their programming's not aimed at us!*"

"How come there's no exit?"

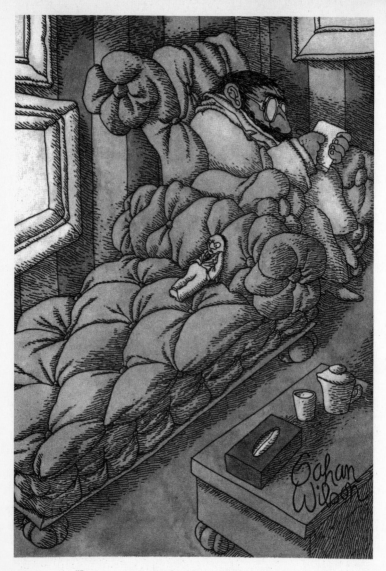

"I suppose my size has something to do with it!"

"I think I've found the trouble, Mr. Nadler!"

"I wish you'd stop wearing that around the house!"

"Mr. Sherman, you hired our team of
management consultants to streamline your enterprise,
and that is precisely what we are doing."

"*Charles!*"

"Gee, Amelia, I'm really very sorry you won't be
able to make it tonight."

"I tell you, Mr. Arthur, this survey has no way of
registering a nonverbal response!"

"You mean to say that you haven't even put your face on yet?"

"Fetch!"

"I'm not talking about your Abominable Snowman, mister—I'm talking about that diamond tiara!"

"My congratulations, professor Moriarty, on a diabolically clever scheme!"

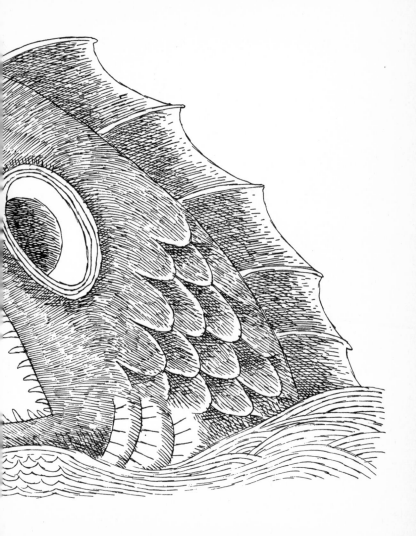

"She sure has big teeth for such a little old lady!"

"I'm a little afraid of what'll happen if we _do_ get him in."

"I understand he's front man for a whole stableful of writers."

"The first rule in mountain climbing is <u>never</u> look down!"

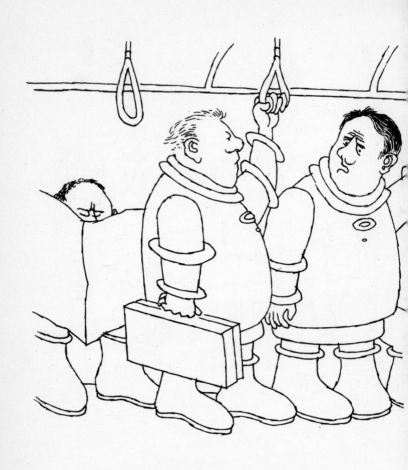

"All the romance has gone out of space travel!"

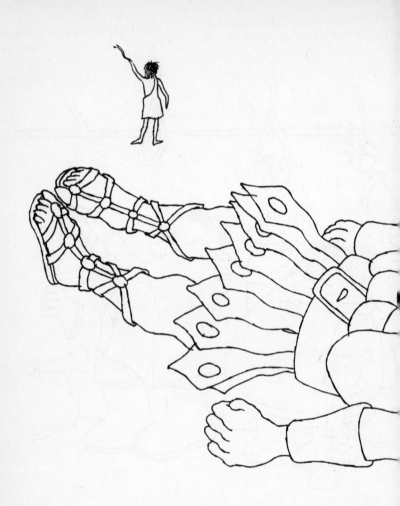

"He'd been doped!"

"You use inferior materials, you get inferior demons."

"It's as I suspected—Mr. Harding, here, is possessed by demons."

"*Still, you've got to admit our being swallowed by
a fish has its humorous aspects!*"

"Harriet—how could you?"

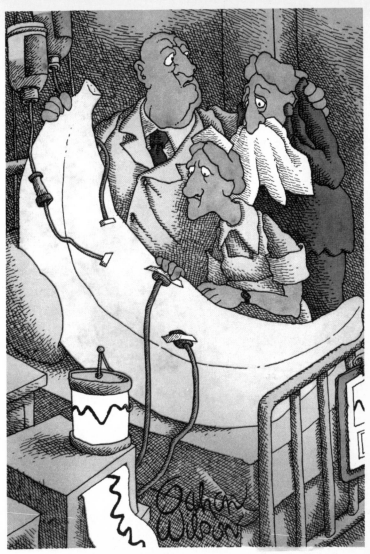

"I'm afraid we'll have no chance of curing your husband until
we find out why he changed into a banana."

"It's new, all right, but it's not very exciting."

"Well, I guess that's the last time the Cullings ever invite <u>us</u> over!"

"Somehow I thought the whole thing would be a lot classier!"

"Is nothing sacred?"

"Sorry, Madame. No dogs are allowed."

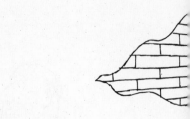

"Shoo! Go away! Shoo!"

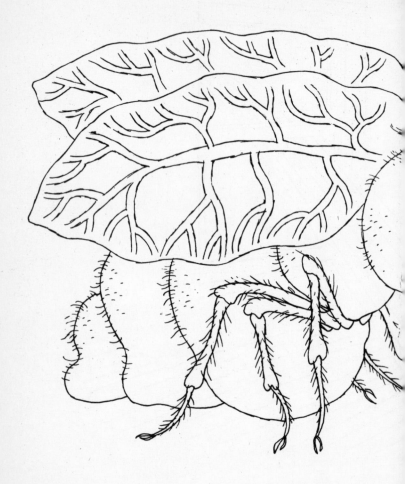

"Get back! Get back!"

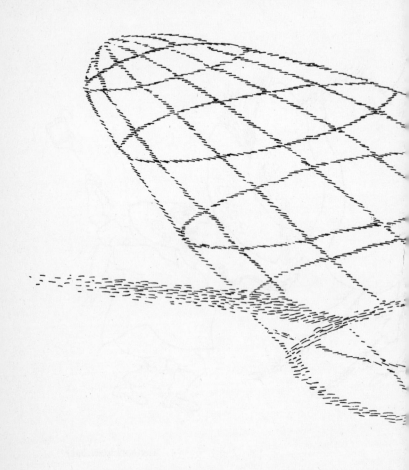

"Oops!"

"Actually I'm afraid we ended up doing a rather more
complicated operation on you than we'd intended."

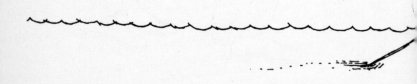

"I've just told Fettle about the will."

"Is it a straight drop to the street?"

"I'm afraid we've bitten off more than we can chew!"

"Name your poison."

"To the lunatic fringe!"

"I remember the very day your father mailed you Claude from Florida."

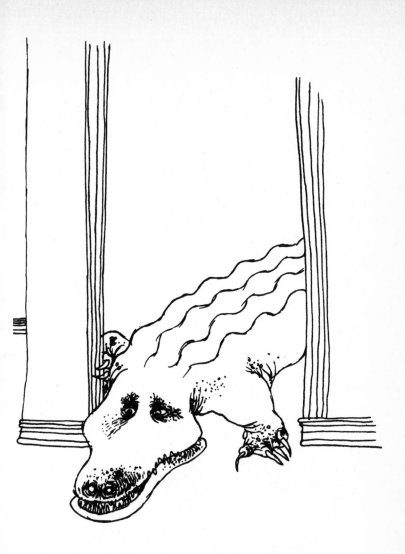

"No, Henry, it is not NASA."

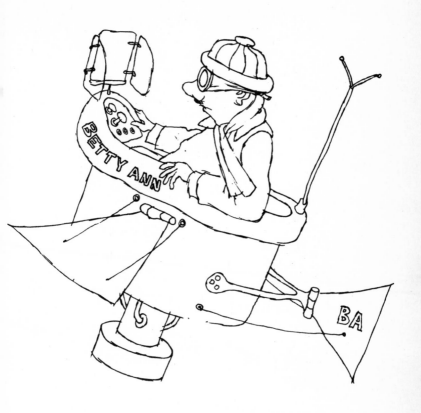

"Oh, I bet he's the fellow who's in all the papers!"

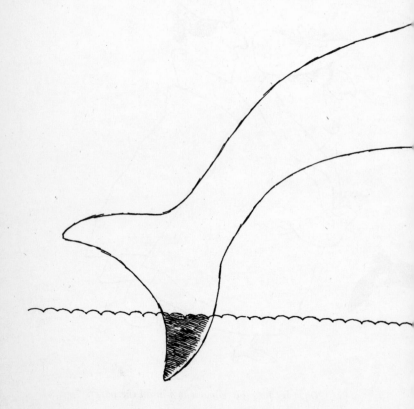

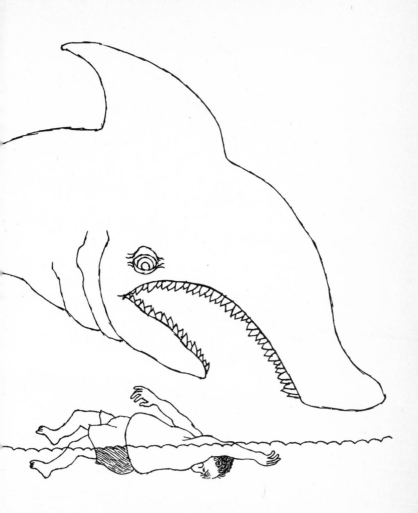

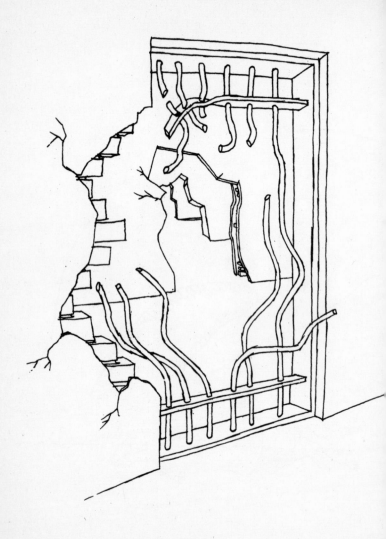

"Frankly, I'm just as glad he's left us."

"You've been with us a long time, Smith . . ."

"Look, Daddy—the first robin!"

"You're a very fine fellow!"

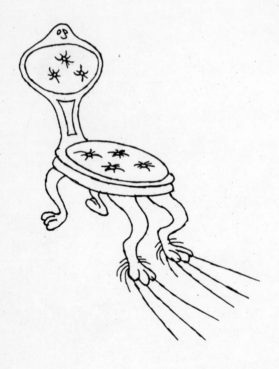

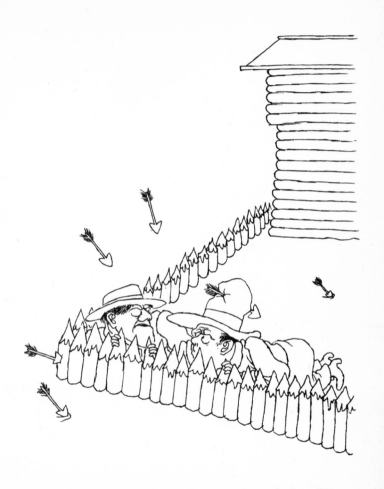

"What idiot suggested economizing on the stockade wall?"

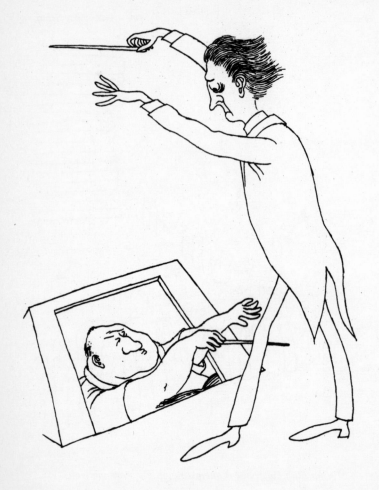

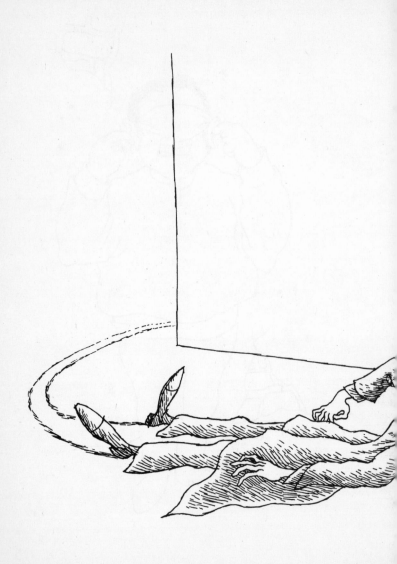

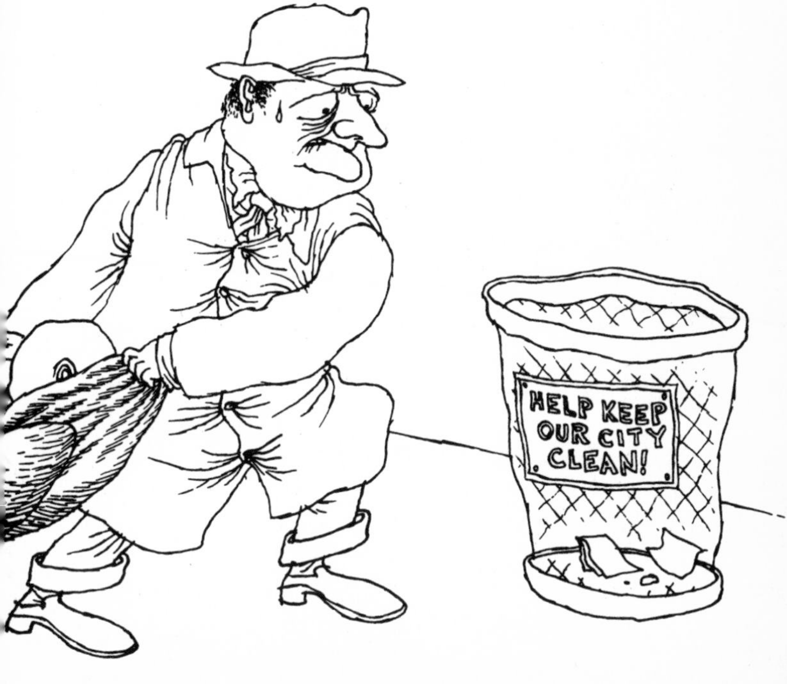
HELP KEEP
OUR CITY
CLEAN!

"I can't make a big noise without you give me a big stick!"

"As a matter of fact, Sir, a three-year-old child did paint it."

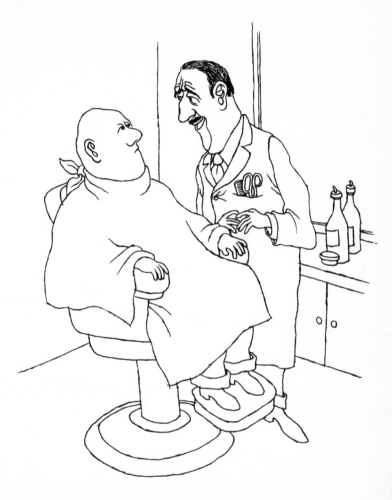

"*Just exactly what was it you wanted me to do, Sir?*"

"My God—I'm being invaded!"

"Matilda, you've forgotten to dust Mr. Harper!"

"His first?"

"Sorry, son, but from now on you're classified."

"It's so pleasant to watch a man who really enjoys his work!"

"There's the curve I was telling you about."

". . . But, whatever else you do,
steer clear of controversial material."

"It said 'Pull,' Mac!"

"Surely we can't have been meant for drudgery such as this!"

"... And how are you feeling today, Ben?"

"*Does this refresh your memory, Doctor?*"

"Maybe this fellow can tell us where we are."

"Ed! Run! It's a trap!"

"Not only is he a good shot, he's a terrible target."

"If only he'd teach us something <u>useful</u>!"

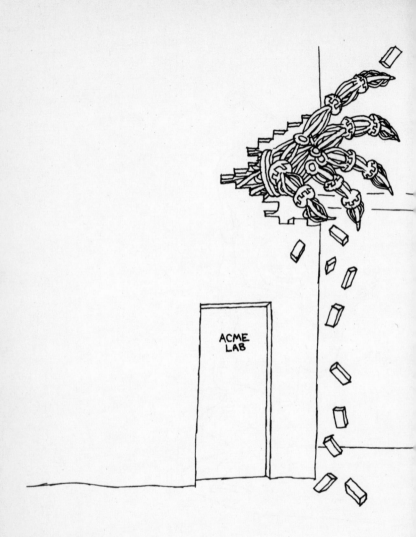

"I can't shake this feeling I've forgotten
to turn something off!"

"Sometimes I wonder if _anything_
would make him happy?"

"The railroad folks have won, Maw,
and it's no use pretending that they haven't."

"*I do believe poor Clem's gone and caught the oak tree blight.*"

"This means war!"

"*Ah* hah!"

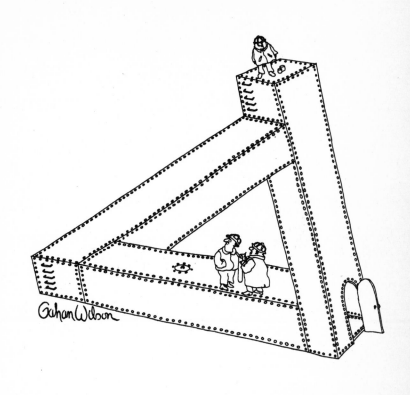

"Let's have another look at the blueprint."

"Just try and tell me this race wasn't fixed!"

"This plea bargaining has really gotten out of hand!"

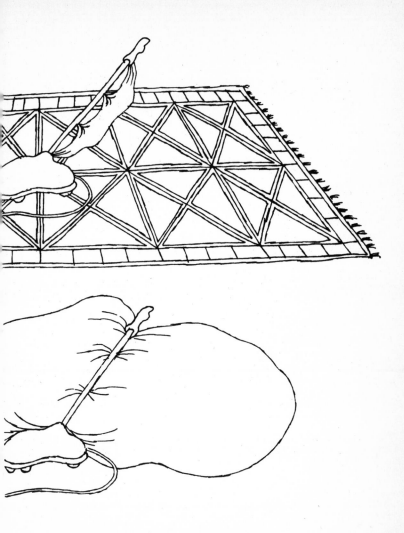

"Why, those aren't my slippers!"

"I guess this is really the big time, Gertrude!"

"The map ends here, too!"

ABOUT THE AUTHOR

GAHAN WILSON says, "I was born dead, and this helped my career almost as much as being the nephew of a lion tamer and a descendant of P.T. Barnum." The first confessed cartoonist to graduate from the Art Institute of Chicago, Wilson has shown at galleries in New York and San Francisco, and his genius for humor has been likened by critics to  that of Swift, Gogol and Twain. His work has appeared in *The New Yorker, Paris Match, Playboy, Punch, Twilight Zone* magazine. *The National Lampoon*, and *The New York Times*.

ALSO AVAILABLE

GAHAN WILSON'S GRAVEDIGGERS PARTY

by Gahan Wilson
ISBN: 0-7434-4548-1

Two-headed pub crawlers and monsters that might be your next-door neighbor are just some of the odd creatures found in the works of Gahan Wilson—the sort of dark and twisted humor that has garnered accolades and awards for this celebrated cartoonist.

Containing over 150 cartoons that stretch across the length of Wilson's ouevre, Gravediggers' Party is a pumpkin-stuffing collection of the weird and the wild, the strange and the super-natural, appreciated by only the most discerning ghoul (and you know who you are).